Rockets

WIZARD'S BOY

The Posh Party

D0489612

MITCHELL POSH
invites
★ ERIC WIZZARD ★
TO HIS BIRTHDAY PARTY
ON SATURDAY at 6·pm.
★ Delicious Food, ★
and Entertainment MUSIC
AT 105 CHATTERINGSIDE Av.
★

Scoular Anderson

A & C Black • London

for Ern and Gaia

Rockets

WIZARD'S BOY – Scoular Anderson

The Muddled Monsters
The Perfect Pizza
The Posh Party
The Potty Panto

First paperback edition 2000
First published 2000 in hardback by
A & C Black (Publishers) Ltd
35 Bedford Row, London WC1R 4JH

The right of Scoular Anderson to be identified as author
and illustrator of this work has been asserted by
him in accordance with the Copyright, Designs
and Patents Act 1988.

ISBN 0-7136-5223-3

A CIP catalogue record for this book is available
from the British Library.

Printed and bound by G. Z. Printek, Bilbao, Spain.

CHAPTER 1

Eric Wizzard, the wizard's boy, came downstairs just as the post arrived. The envelopes landed on the mat.

The last envelope was too big to come right through.

Eric opened the door and gave the big envelope a good tug.

Out it came, and the letterbox snapped shut.

'Hey! Steady on! Steady on!'
shouted the door-knocker.
(This was a wizard's house after all.)

Eric slammed
the door.

Eric looked at the huge envelope.
It was addressed to him and he
had been waiting for it all week.
He opened it up.

Eric felt a warm glow in his tummy.
Everyone in his class had invitations
already. Eric thought he'd been
missed out.

He rushed down the hall.

His heart sank when he saw his mum's case on the table.

Eric's mum was an airline pilot and she was always dashing around the world.

Where are you going?

South America.

8

9

In the kitchen, Eric's dad had just tried
to open a cereal packet by magic.
His spell was supposed to be
'Rip off the top bit!'

But instead, he got *'Lift off into orbit!'*

Eric's dad was a hopeless wizard.

Now the Crunchie Crinkles were
whizzing round the light like
asteroids round the sun.
Eric's dad was up a stepladder trying
to catch them with a sieve.

Eric's dad came down from the stepladder.

At that moment Eric just knew that the last thing he wanted was to be driven up to Mitchell Posh's house by his dad.
He would die of embarrassment.

CHAPTER 2

The day of Mitchell Posh's party arrived.
Eric lay in bed and tried to think how
he could get to the party without his dad.

There was nothing for it. His dad would have to drive him. Perhaps he could get him to wear a suit like a chauffeur! But Eric didn't think Dad owned a suit.

'Never mind Dad's clothes!'
thought Eric. 'What about
my own party shirt?'

He leapt out of bed...

...he rummaged
in a drawer...

...and he pulled
out his best shirt.
It was crumpled
and had a big
stain on it.

He rushed downstairs.

His dad preferred to do things by magic
but his spells hardly ever worked.
Eric checked that the shirt really
went into the machine.

Then he dashed to the shops to buy
a present for Mitchell.

He settled on a
model boat.

When Eric got home, his dad was up the stepladder again.

Eric looked up and saw his best shirt
floating round the ceiling.
It was accompanied by two pairs of
socks, a pair of underpants and a hanky.

Eric's dad came down from the
stepladder.

Eric came downstairs dressed
for the party. The flying
shirt made him
feel very light.

He could see that his dad wasn't much
good at wrapping things. Mitchell's
present was in the lumpiest parcel he
had ever seen. He was sure it moved
when he touched it.

Okay, let's go!

CHAPTER 3

Eric and his dad set off for the party. Theodore the dog came as well. Eric worried about what the Poshes would think of Dad's multicoloured car.

(His dad had once tried to get rid of a mark on the seat, but the spell *'Stain go!'* became *'Rainbow'* instead.)

To make matters worse, Dad drove right up to the door of 105 Chatteringside Avenue. Everyone stared. Mitchell Posh and his mum were standing by the front door. Mitchell was looking very smart and his mum was looking Eric's dad up and down.

Eric offered Mitchell the lumpy parcel.

'Not yet!' snapped Mitchell's mum,
and she snatched the parcel from him.

This must go
to the presents
room...

... to be opened
with the others
after the magician's
act which...

Mitchell's mum was
interrupted because
at that moment
the parcel definitely
gave a little jump.

Mitchell grabbed his present
before his mum could say anything.

Mitchell's mum was
interrupted again.

She dashed into the house.

29

Mitchell's mum slammed down the phone and clasped her hand to her head.

Then to Eric's horror, his dad made
a suggestion.

So Eric had to help his dad carry the magician's box into the sitting-room.

Eric knew a party magician and a wizard were not the same thing. He just hoped his dad knew some simple card tricks.

CHAPTER 4

Eric's dad opened up the magician's box and pulled out a few things.

Just then, Eric saw something across the hall.

He ran after the dog but he seemed to have disappeared.

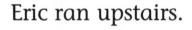

Eric ran upstairs.

He searched every room.

He came downstairs again.

He looked in
the kitchen…

...before running
out into the garden.

Then he came
back inside and…

...dashed into the dining-room…

Theodore was eating Mitchell Posh's grand birthday cake.

Eric called to his dad. He would have to ask him to do some magic.

His dad thought for a moment.

Eric knew he should never have asked his dad to do magic.

With difficulty Eric locked Theodore the snake in the car. When he came back he heard lots of cheering and laughing coming from the sitting-room.

He went to see what was happening. His dad had started trying out some magic tricks...

...and the magic tricks were not the usual kind.

Eric was glad his dad hadn't got round to sawing Mrs Posh in half yet.

Then Eric caught sight of Mitchell
out in the garden.

Eric went out to join him.

Then Eric remembered that his dad had wrapped the present.

Dad had obviously used magic...

...and got it wrong, as usual.

Mitchell's mum came into the garden.
She looked rather dazed.

Then Eric's shirt tried to fly again
and that was too much for her.

So the children helped themselves to tea
and no one noticed the half-eaten cake.

CHAPTER 5

By the time Eric and his dad got home, the magic had just about worn off.

Even Theodore was beginning to feel like his old self again.

Eric's mum had already arrived.

Eric was pleased that life was never dull
with a dad who was a hopeless wizard.